# Presidents' Day

SIMON SPOTLIGHT
An imprint of Simon & Schuster Children's Publishing Division
1230 Avenue of the Americas, New York, NY 10020
This Simon Spotlight edition December 2021
First Aladdin Paperbacks edition January 2010
Text copyright © 2010 by Margaret McNamara
Illustrations copyright © 2010 by Mike Gordon
For information about special discounts for bulk purchases, please contact
Simon & Schuster Special Sales at 1-866-506-1949 or business@simonandschuster.com.
Manufactured in the United States of America 1021 LAK
2 4 6 8 10 9 7 5 3 1
Cataloging-in-Publication Data was previously supplied for the paperback edition of this
title from the Library of Congress.
Library of Congress Cataloging-in-Publication Data
McNamara, Margaret. Presidents' Day / by Margaret McNamara ; illustrated by Mike
Gordon. — 1st Aladdin Paperbacks ed. p. cm. — (Ready-to-read) Summary: In February,
the first-graders in Mrs. Connor's class present facts about the presidents.
[1. Presidents—Fiction. 2. Presidents' Day—Fiction. 3. Schools—Fiction.]
I. Gordon, Mike, 1948 Mar. 16- ill.
II. Title. PZ7.M47879343Pr 2010
[E]—dc22 2009023715
ISBN 978-1-5344-9894-5 (hc)
ISBN 978-1-4169-9170-0 (pbk)
ISBN 978-1-4814-6859-6 (ebook)

# Presidents' Day

written by Margaret McNamara
illustrated by Mike Gordon

Ready-to-Read

Simon Spotlight
New York   London   Toronto   Sydney   New Delhi

"Who has a birthday soon?"
asked Mrs. Connor.
"I do!" said Ayanna.

"Another famous person
was born on that day,"
said Mrs. Connor.

"You?" asked Michael.

"Abraham Lincoln!"
said Ayanna.

Ayanna knew a lot about
Abraham Lincoln.
"He was a great
president," she said.

"What is a president?"
asked Reza.

All that week the first graders learned about the presidents.

"The president is in charge of America," said Michael.

"Like the principal!" said Reza.

"When we get older,"
said Hannah,
"we will vote to choose
our president."

"*Not* like the principal!"
said Reza.

"The president lives
in the White House,"
said Neil.

"That is a very big house!"
said Jamie.

"The first president was
George Washington,"
said Katie.

"He was good at math,"
said Eigen.

"President Tyler had fifteen children!" said Emma.

"Teddy bears were named after Teddy Roosevelt," said James.

"President Reagan was a movie star before he was a president!" said Becky.

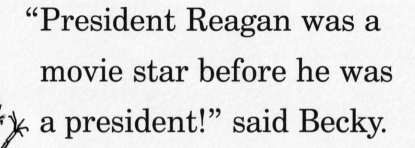

"Our president is
Barack Obama!"
said Nia.

"Abraham Lincoln was tall
and a little funny looking,"
Ayanna said.

"But he was very wise.
He read lots of books."

"He stopped Americans from fighting against one another."

"He thought all people were equal."

"When I grow up,
I want to be a president,
just like Lincoln,"
said Ayanna.

"When you grow up,
I think you will,"
said Mrs. Connor.